The Bedtime Spell

Written by Joni Kennedy & Brooke Motes

Illustrated by Carrie Sills

For Jane, Jet, and Bayler, who always have itchy backs—Joni K.

For my kids—Brooke M.

For my grandkids, Blake and Lauren---Carrie S.

THE BEDTIME SPELL

By Joni Kennedy & Brooke Motes

Illustrated by Carrie Sills

Freddy Flanagan was tucked into bed,
with blankets warm and pillow red.

His frizzy orange hair was wild with curls,
and his teeth when he smiled were white
like pearls.

The sun slowly set in the summer sky,
the twinkling stars appeared up high.

Down softly sat Mrs. Flanagan by Freddy,
she gave him a kiss, a hug and a teddy.

Freddy performed a prize-winning yawn, then off went the lights and his mother was gone.

Silent and still Freddy
laid in bed,
counting the sheep
jumping over his head.

Next he played the quiet game,

but playing alone just wasn't the same.

He called for his mom to play the game too,
Mrs. Flanagan wondered what else she
could do.

Her face lit up with a clever grin,
she grabbed a book and then walked in.

She whispered the words,
"Abracadabra, Kaboom!"
That's when the magic filled the room!

A HANDBOOK OF
MAGIC, SPELLS
AND
POTIONS

"To fall into enchanted sleep,
roll on your belly and don't make a peep."

"Close your eyes and I'll tell you the spell:
First take an egg and crack the shell."

"Down your back the yolk will spread,"

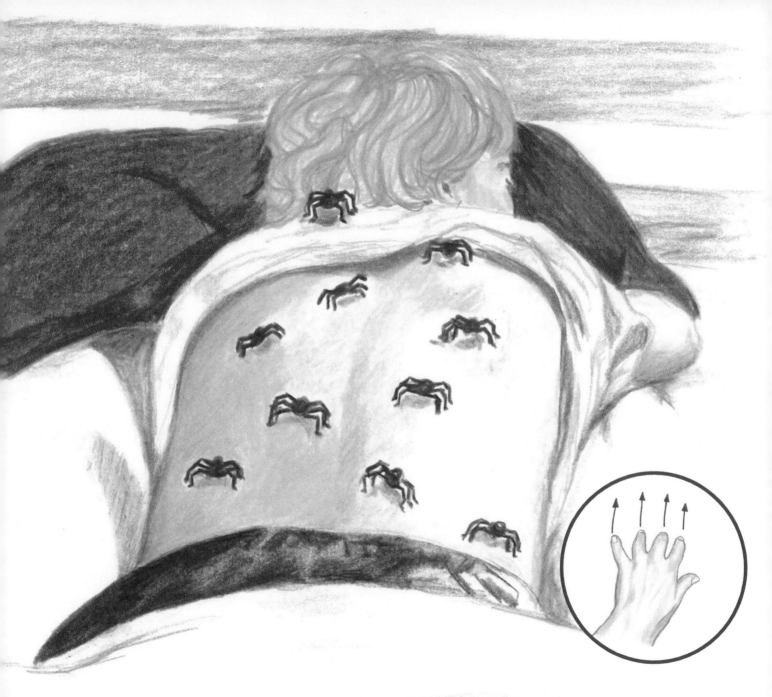

"10 spiders crawl up to your head."

"9 birds peck down your spine,"

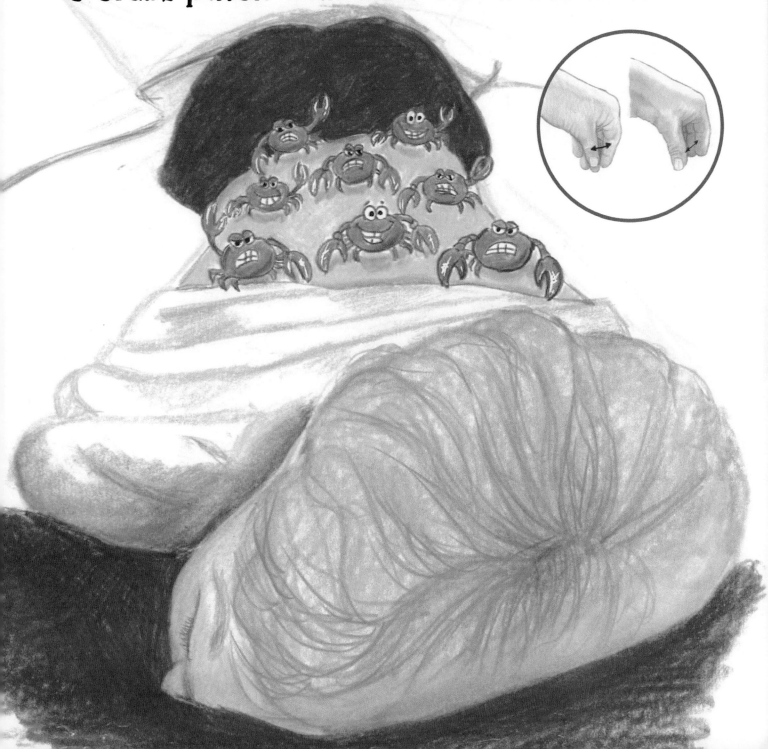

"8 crabs pinch with their claws that shine."

"7 snakes slither with nowhere to hide,"

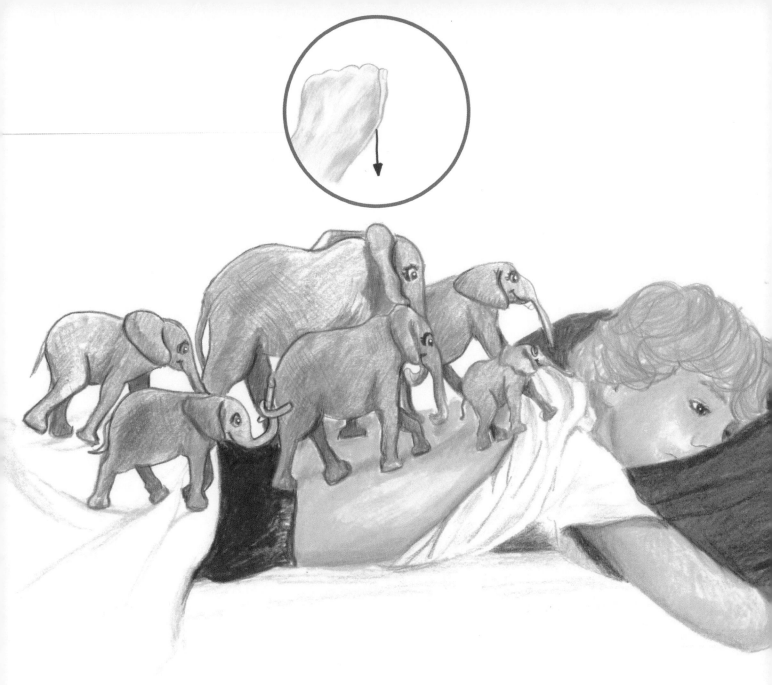

"6 elephants stomp along with pride."

"5 monkeys swing to and fro,"

"2 tigers scratch without a tear."

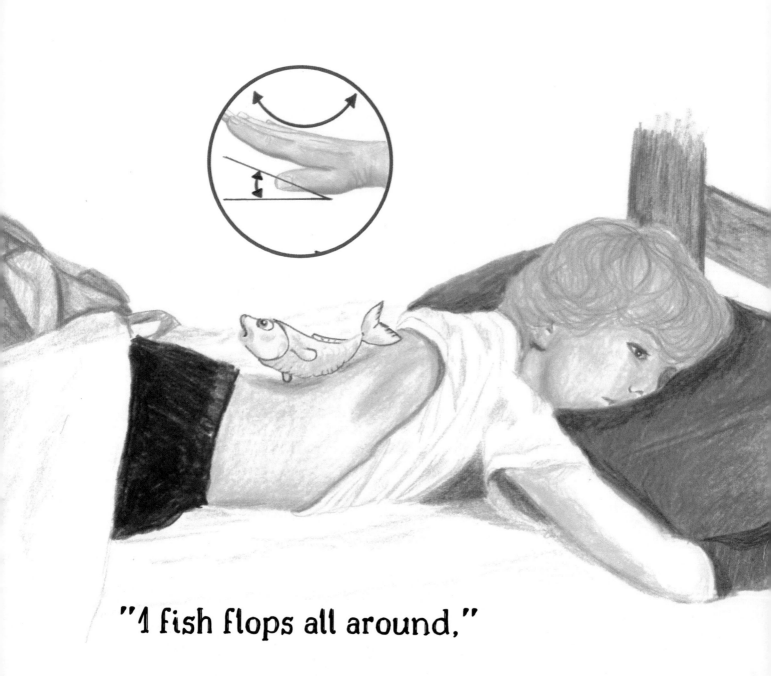

"1 fish flops all around,"

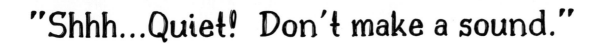

"Shhh...Quiet! Don't make a sound."

"Then there comes a cooling breeze,
all the creatures have to freeze.
Now it's time for sleepy please!"

But Freddy was already catching some Z's,
(just like the spell guarantees)

His mother tiptoed out of the room,
and replaced the book next to her broom.

She went to her room and turned out
the light,
uttering the last word of the spell:
"GOOD NIGHT!"

Check out these other books by the Author:

18 Lists Every Mom Needs

Scribble Masterpieces: Turn Scribbles into Art

If You're Sleepy and You Know It

The Mean Grumpy Old Hen

Printed in Great Britain
by Amazon

19361689R00020